To Freddy Bee and Teddy Tee
I dedicate this fantasy.
(And just in case you hate arcana –
that's Frederick Bowden and Edward Traynor) – I.W

For Porthleven School - R.A

First published in paperback in Great Britain by HarperCollins Children's Books in 2006

1 3 5 7 9 10 8 6 4 2
ISBN -13: 978-0-00-713124-2
ISBN -10: 0-00-713124-0

HarperCollins Children's Books is a division of HarperCollins Publishers Ltd.

Text copyright © Ian Whybrow 2006
Illustrations copyright © Russell Ayto 2006

Visit our website at: www.harpercollinschildrensbooks.co.uk

Printed in Singapore

TIM, TED & THE
PIRATES

Ian Whybrow illustrated by Russell Ayto

HarperCollins *Children's Books*

This is the school where Tim goes.
This is his teacher, Miss Wait.

Looks like it's time for a story –
"Off we go - in line - keep straight!"

Tim and his Ted sit up nicely, wondering which it'll be.

"Today," says Miss Wait, "will be special.
There's a drink and a lovely surprise.

We're going to read
Little Bear's Daring Deed."
Tim and his Ted close their eyes.

Miss Wait reads –
the room fills with water.

A dolphin glides in
through the door.

He invites Ted and Tim
to go for a swim,

And off they all go
to explore.

Tim and Ted ride along to Loot Island
where pirates are up to no good.

But suddenly - CRUNCH! -
a shark eats them for lunch.

With a nice treasure chest
for his pud!

It's lucky that Tim
finds a flashlight,
because now he can
easily look.

And soon - what a pleasure! -
Tim can see heaps of treasure!
Look out!
Here's a line and a hook!

The hook catches hold
of the chest full of gold.

"Yo-ho," yell the pirates.
"A bite!"

Ted shouts with a roar,
"Quick, Tim, hold my paw!
And everyone else hang
on tight!"

The captain says,
"Heave-ho me hearties!
We'll soon have our gold
back on deck!"

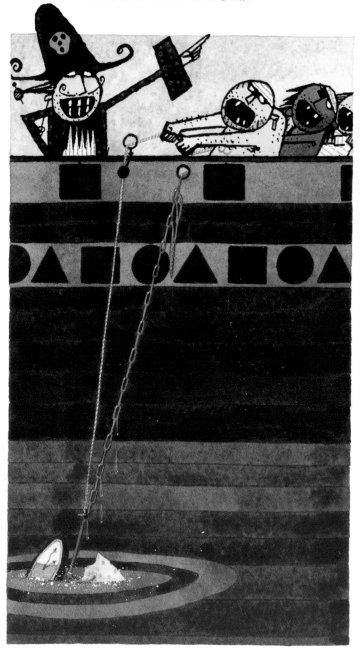

When they see what pops out,

the pirates all shout:

"What's that?

It's a **monster!**

Oo heck!"

"Hands up!" orders Ted,
"and surrender!"

"It's a bear!" yells the Mate.
"Well, I'm blessed!"

"We're going to set sail and put you in jail!"
shouts Tim, "So you're *under arrest!*"

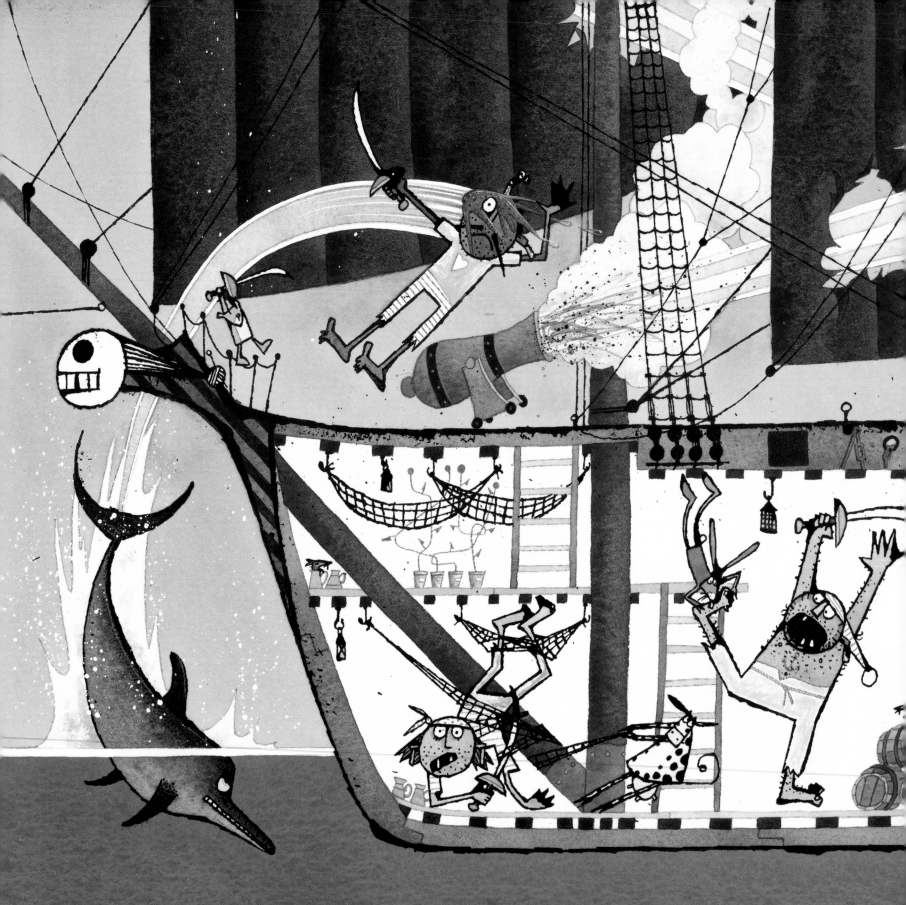

"We'll never give up!" scream the pirates.

And cutlasses clatter and clash.

Then that bad pirate crew and their mad captain too
end up walking the plank with a ...

"Look out, Tim! You've knocked your drink over!
Let me get you a cloth!" cries Miss Wait.
"It's all on the floor, look! Oh dear, here's some more.
My goodness, you are in a state!"

At home time Mum asks, "How was school dear?"
Tim says, "Oh, we didn't do much.
Only reading and writing and stories and fighting
and capturing pirates and such!"

Look out for more fantastic books by Ian Whybrow and Russell Ayto!

Little Wolf and Smellybreff

Badness for Beginners

Ian Whybrow + Tony Ross

Paperback:
0-00-714361-3

Book and Audio CD:
0-00-721302-6

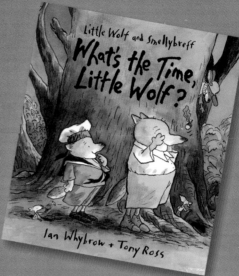

Little Wolf and Smellybreff

What's the Time, Little Wolf?

Ian Whybrow + Tony Ross

Paperback:
0-00-714362-1

Book and Audio CD:
0-00-721512-6

Paperback:
0-00-664726-X

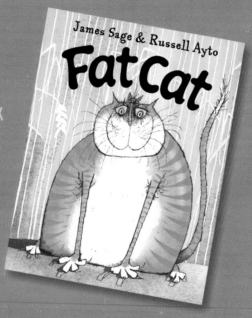

James Sage & Russell Ayto

Fat Cat

Hardback:
0-00-710393-X

Paperback:
0-00-710394-8

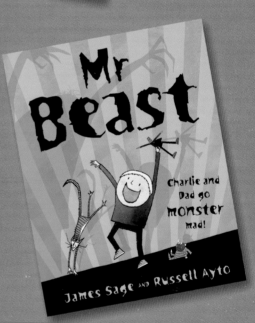

Mr Beast

Charlie and Dad go **monster** mad!

James Sage and Russell Ayto

For more information on these and other HarperCollins picture books,
visit our website at: www.harpercollinschildrensbooks.co.uk

HarperCollins *Children's Books*